RAINY DAY TOGETHER

by Ellen Parsons

Pictures by Lillian Hoban

Harper & Row, Publishers

New York, Evanston, San Francisco, London

Parsons
C.S ENDICOTT

RAINY DAY TOGETHER
Text copyright © 1971 by Ellen Parsons
Pictures copyright © 1971 by Lillian Hoban

Printed in the United States of America. For information address
Harper & Row, Publishers, Inc., 49 East 33rd Street, New York, N.Y.
10016. Published simultaneously in Canada by Fitzhenry & Whiteside
Limited, Toronto.
Library of Congress Catalog Card Number: 72-135781
Standard Book Number: Trade edition 06-024687-1
Harpercrest edition 06-024688-X

RAINY DAY TOGETHER

Mommy is at the window
ironing a long dark grey dress for her
because it's a cold, rainy day.
Mine's long too, but green.
We put on our dresses
and go to the bathroom.
She sits first, cause the seat is cold.
Then when I sit, it's warm.

Then we go to the kitchen.
She has coffee, I have coffee-milk.
We both have an egg
and an apricot Danish.
We watch the rain through the window
making bubbles
from falling so hard on the garden path.
It will be a good day.
She washes the dishes, I dry them.

Then we go upstairs and make our beds.
She comes in my room
and reads to me for a while,
three chapters from a long book.
And then I sit on the clean wood floor
and play dolls,
while she sits on the bed
and writes letters
on a record cover balanced on her knee.
"Who are you writing to?"
"Just old friends."

My mommy is very pretty.
She doesn't wear makeup
or put curlers in her hair
or ever make TV dinners.
She finishes her letter and says,
"Let's go downstairs
and get some lunch."
So we do.

Vegetable soup
and bacon-lettuce-and-tomato sandwich
on brown bread
and milk and oatmeal cookies.
While I eat,
she tells me about her old friends.
"You've never met them
and they've never met you."

"They live in a big white house in the country
with two other families
and a dog and cat and puppies and a goat
and two children, a boy and a girl, your age.

They have a long swing outside
and a vegetable garden.
They were my friends from school.
You'll like them and they'll like you."

"And they want you and me and Daddy
to come there soon."

Daddy.
Daddy will be home in a very few hours,
at six thirty.

We eat our cookies
in the same way—
around to the center
where a nut is.

We wash our dishes again.
She washes, I dry.
We play a game of sitting on the floor
and looking at each other
without saying anything.
And pretty soon we start laughing.
That's fun too.

It's still raining.
Our toes are cold,
so we put on our fuzzy slippers.
Hers are purple, mine are orange.
Then we build a huge Tinkertoy house.

And I brush her hair and she brushes mine.
We don't pull.

Then we go and start a fire
in the fireplace.
And she puts supper on,
chicken cheese casserole.
Everything is baked together in one pot
so the flavors mix.
She puts in some wine.
It smells good.
Now it has to cook in the oven for a while.

So we go to the living room,
and the fire is burning and snapping.
We toast our toes.
She reads to me again,
two chapters, and then—

open-close-BANG
and I run to Daddy.
He puts down some wood
he has to make a bookcase with.

His raincoat is dark and wet.
His hair and beard are curly and wet.
His face is pink with cold.

I hug that wetness.
He picks me up and hugs me hard
and kisses me.
"Where's Mommy?"
I look her way.

And she's standing in the doorway
and there's firelight behind her
and her hair is long and dark and wavy,

and they look at each other
and walk towards each other

and hug
very hard.